THIS BOOK WAS DESIGNED FOR DIFFICULTY LEVELS FROM BEGINNER TO HARD. CARVING MASTERS AND PROFESSIONALS MAY FIND THE DESIGNS EASY. HOWEVER, ALL CREATORS WILL ENJOY MAKING THEIR PUMPKINS UNIQUE BY ADDING DETAILS, TEXTURES, OR ADDITIONAL ART. CHILDREN SHOULD BE SUPERVISED AND TOOLS BE USED AT YOUR OWN DISCRETION.

INSTRUCTIONS:

1. CUT THE TOP, BOTTOM, OR SIDE OFF OF YOUR PUMPKIN AND SCRAPE OUT THE INSIDES.

2. THEN, SIMPLY CUT OUT THE DESIGN YOU WANT TO USE AND TAPE IT TO YOUR DRY PUMPKIN.

3. USING A PEN, FIRMLY TRACE THE IMAGE SO THAT IT SHOWS ON THE PUMPKIN'S SKIN.

4. CUT OUT THE BLACK AREAS IN THE DESIGN.

5. ADD A CANDLE OR LIGHT, AND ENJOY!

CARVING TIPS:

✦ SOME PEOPLE PREFER TO CUT THE TOP OFF OF THE PUMPKIN WHILE OTHERS PREFER TO CUT THE BOTTOM OR EVEN THE BACK. CHOOSE A METHOD THAT IS BEST FOR YOUR PUMPKIN AND ART.

✦ USE TOOLS THAT WORK BEST FOR YOU. SPOONS ARE GREAT FOR REMOVING PUMPKIN SEEDS AND INSIDES. STEAK, PARING, AND EXACTO KNIVES WORK WELL FOR CARVING, AS WELL AS SAWS, CHISELS, AND ROTARY TOOLS.

✦ CARVING IN LAYERS OR DIFFERENT DEPTHS WILL ALLOW THE LIGHT TO SHINE THROUGH YOUR PUMPKIN WITH DIFFERENT SHADES.

✦ YOU CAN ADD DETAILS TO YOUR CARVING DESIGNS WITH RASPS, ZESTERS, WOOD CARVING OR SCULPTING TOOLS.

✦ TO HELP PROLONG YOUR JACK-O-LANTERN'S LIFE, YOU CAN ADD LEMON JUICE TO THE CUTOUT AREAS, KEEP IN A COOL PLACE, AND WRAP IT WITH PLASTIC WRAP WHEN IT'S NOT BEING USED.

HAVE FUN!

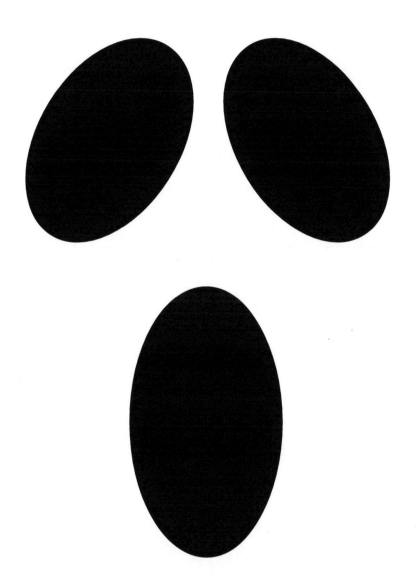

13

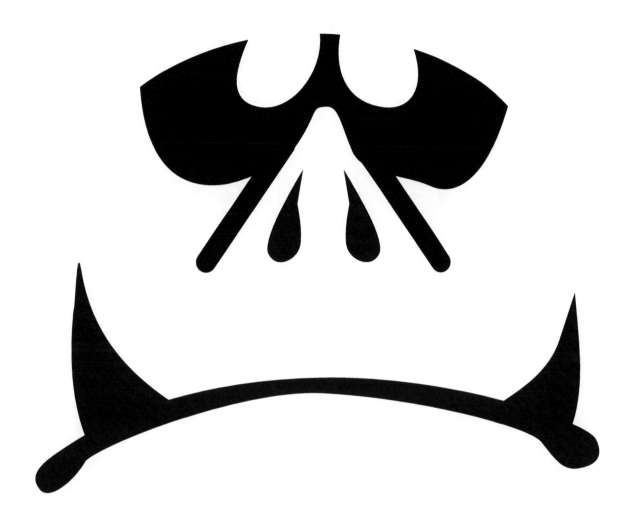

49

59

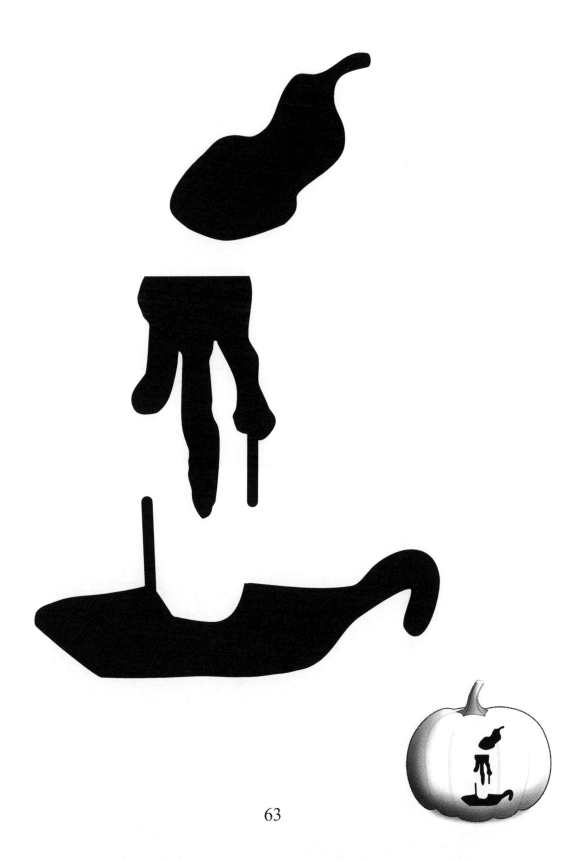

83

BOO!
OR
BOO!

99

101

FROM THE AUTHOR:

I hope you enjoyed this book and creating your pumpkin masterpiece!

I would love to see a review!

However, if you want to contact me personally for feedback my email is healthyhappyfarm@gmail.com or visit me at HealthyHappyFarm.com

Thank you for your support and Happy Halloween!

Made in the USA
Coppell, TX
13 October 2020